Patch and Parker were pirates.

They had the same
treasure map!

Patch dug for
the treasure.

Parker dug for
the treasure.

They found the
treasure chest.

"We don't want to share!" they said.

The treasure was
melting.

"We can share!"
said Patch.

17

"Sharing can be fun!"
they said.

Puzzle Time

Can you find these
pictures in the story?

Which pages are the
pictures from?

Turn over for answers!

Answers

The pictures come from these pages:

a. pages 14–15

b. pages 6–7

c. pages 4–5

d. pages 10–11

First published in 2014 by
Franklin Watts
338 Euston Road
London
NW1 3BH

Franklin Watts Australia
Level 17/207 Kent Street
Sydney
NSW 2000

Text © Clare De Marco 2014
Illustration © Nicola Anderson 2014

A CIP catalogue record for this book is available from the British Library.

ISBN 978 1 4451 3222 8 (hbk)
ISBN 978 1 4451 3223 5 (pbk)
ISBN 978 1 4451 3224 2 (ebook)
ISBN 978 1 4451 3225 9 (library ebook)

Series Editor: Jackie Hamley
Editor: Melanie Palmer
Series Advisor: Catherine Glavina
Series Designer: Peter Scoulding

Printed in China

Franklin Watts is a division of Hachette Children's Books,
an Hachette UK company. www.hachette.co.uk